Sure As Sunrise

Stories of Bruh Rabbit & His Walkin' Talkin' Friends

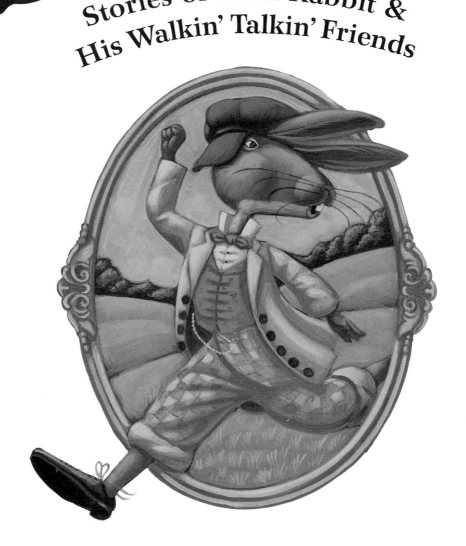

Alice McGill illustrated by **Don Tate**

Houghton Mifflin Company Boston 2004

To Little Darryl, my grandson, and to all children and grownups
alike that enjoy listening to and telling long-ago stories.

Special thanks to my editors, Amy Flynn and Ann Rider, for encouraging me
to bridge the gap between telling stories and writing stories successfully.
—A. M.

I thank God.

To the art and editorial staff at Perfection Learning Corporation, who provided
me with the first open door into the world of children's literature.
—D. T.

www.houghtonmifflinbooks.com

The text of this book is set in Wilke. The art is acrylic paint on textured paper.

Library of Congress Cataloging-in-Publication Data
McGill, Alice.
Sure as sunrise : stories of Bruh Rabbit and his walkin' talkin' friends / by Alice McGill ; illustrated by Don Tate.
p. cm.
Contents: Please don't fling me in the briar patch—Bruh Possum and the snake—How the
critters got groceries—Bruh Rabbit's mystery bag—Looking to get married.
ISBN 0-618-21196-9
1. African Americans—Folklore. 2. Tales—United States. [1. African Americans—Folklore.
2. Animals—Folklore. 3. Folklore—United States.]
I. Tate, Don, ill. II. Title.
PZ8.1.M1713Su 2004   398.2'089'96073—dc22   2003012289

Printed in Singapore
TWP 10 9 8 7 6 5 4 3 2 1

Contents

✺ Introduction ✺

WHEN I WAS GROWING UP IN HALIFAX COUNTY, NORTH CAROLINA, MANY SMALL FARMING communities sponsored a quartet competition called the Great Battle of Songs. Folks lined up at schoolhouse doors to hear the best singers. Tickets cost twenty cents for grownups and ten cents for children.

Often the lead singers introduced the songs with a short story about creatures such as Sis Possum and Bruh Rabbit who were "from the time of way back yonder." I cannot remember the lead singers' names, but I shall never forget their words and songs which helped to influence this small collection of read-aloud stories: *Sure As Sunrise: Stories of Bruh Rabbit and His Walkin' Talkin' Friends*.

Years later, I graduated from a state teachers' college in North Carolina. During my sophomore year, an American literature professor often challenged her students to "apprise" themselves of general knowledge by exchanging and discussing little- and well-known facts about the world at large.

During one of these apprising sessions, a fellow classmate stated that Joel Chandler Harris was the creator of the Bruh Rabbit stories. At that time, folktales were not included in the American literature course outline. I had never heard of Joel Chandler Harris so I made a note to search for his name in the library. At the same time, I did not believe my classmate, and I told her so. How could any one person have created the Bruh Rabbit stories? I challenged her.

She was ready for me with names, dates, times, and places. She had seen the 1946 movie about Uncle Remus.

I then read Harris's book, *Uncle Remus: His Songs and Sayings,* which had been published in 1880. I found many similarities between his Uncle Remus stories about Bruh Rabbit and the stories I had heard as a child. However, Harris's dialect was unlike any I knew and was difficult to read aloud in rhythmic patterns. Also, it seemed to me that Uncle Remus spoke a whole mouth full of words to describe a simple incident, whereas our neighbor, Neptune Clark, would use just two words to paint a picture.

Mister Nep, as we called him, was an old man when he and his older sibling, Sis Mashanna, moved down the road from my family in Mary's Chapel. Instantly, his front porch became a living stage for him to act out stories about Bruh Rabbit, Bruh Possum, and Bruh Fox.

Mister Nep's rendition of "Please Don't Fling Me in the Briar Patch" led me to believe that he was an eyewitness to the goings-on of fascinating creatures. I learned first-person storytelling from him. My siblings and I laughed and clapped every time Bruh Rabbit outwitted big Bruh Bear or sneaky Bruh Fox. Of course, we requested this story about a hundred times. We could imagine how high, how wide, or how far a critter's world stretched when Mister Nep merely stated, "Bruh Rabbit lived b'twix earth and sky."

To us, these creatures shared many of our own experiences. Just as Bruh Bear packed food, my mother often packed cheese and bread, or sardines and soda crackers, or sweet potatoes and streak-of-lean pork to take to the cotton field for our noontime dinner. This practice kept us from having to walk a long way home and back. Over time, many daylight hours were saved for picking cotton. And we would miss fewer days from school. Life was hard sometimes. Sometimes, life was good—as good as Mister Nep's stories.

I learned later that during and after the middle passage of enslaved Africans, Bruh Rabbit became a spokesperson for these oppressed people. Hailing from Africa as Waikama, a hare, he dared to defy the king under his new title, "Bruh Rabbit." This little character adapted to new surroundings, and the enslaved could express their hopes and disappointments through his wit and trickery. His words passed from one plantation to another, picking up new tellers and new listeners.

Word-of-mouth stories can easily die after the teller's eyes have closed. Modern-day folklorists agree that African Americans did not really speak the language Joel Chandler Harris created for Uncle Remus. However, had it not been for Harris, much of the legacy of Bruh Rabbit might have been lost.

When I was a child my father's Bruh Rabbit stories were so real that I often thought I would, one day, meet this witty character, dressed in baggy britches with a watch chain dangling from his vest pocket. No other critter could match Bruh Rabbit's tricks or his good sense in following the rules of survival. Victory for him was as sure as sunrise.

Please Don't Fling Me in the Briar Patch

Bruh meant "brother" and Sis meant "sister" in the African American dialect. The early African Americans gave one another these titles to show that they were tied together by friendship and respect.

NOT TOO MANY FOLKS KNOW THIS, BUT BRUH RABBIT CAN'T SING A LICK. The few that ever heard him trying to put a tune in his voice said he sounded like somebody was sticking a pin in his hide. I think Bruh Rabbit was ashamed 'cause he couldn't sing. He sure did love to hear good singing, though. Folks knew that by the way he took to thumping his foot when he happened to hear other folks' good singing.

Well, Bruh Rabbit's bad singing is not my business, but I do want to tell you about the day he got caught because of his love of song.

Early one morning, Bruh Rabbit sat on his do-nothing stool, waiting for Mister Man to leave home. He was planning on eating fall turnips from Mister Man's garden.

That's the same morning he spied Bruh Bear coming along with a big yellow kerchief tied to the end of his grubbing hoe. Sis Possum, Sis

Dog, and Bruh Fox trailed along behind him, toting hoes and such. All of 'em had on work clothes for clearing new ground. That's when you use hoes and grubbing hoes to chop down in-the-way bushes and grub in-the-way roots out of the ground.

Bruh Rabbit nodded his head in greeting, as they got closer. But you know they passed him by and nary one of 'em so much as cracked a lip to him? Bruh Rabbit thought they didn't have no manners.

Then Bruh Bear broke off from the rest and tied that big yellow kerchief full of something to a high-up oak tree limb. He followed the others to the far end of the woods.

Bruh Rabbit stood up, yawned, and stretched himself. Slow-like, he inched his body toward the tree. At last, he was standing right under the kerchief.

Something smelled so good, Bruh Rabbit jumped up and down, trying to reach the kerchief, but he couldn't. His knees commenced to feeling weak from jumping so much. Finally, he climbed the tree and crawled out on the limb and loosened the knot. That did it! He and the kerchief fell to the ground at the same time.

Quicker than you can say "little piece of cornbread layin' on the shelf," that kerchief was laid open. There, spread before Bruh Rabbit, was the biggest cake of delicious cheese and the softest loaf of bread still warm from the ashes.

You guessed right. Bruh Rabbit made that dinner his very own. Now, there was enough to feed four folks, but he ate it all in minutes. By dinnertime, he was curled up to sleep in the thicket.

Now, you can't picture what them hungry critters looked like at dinnertime when they saw that scrunched-up kerchief lying on the ground. Bruh Bear kept reaching at the limb like the something-to-eat was still there. Sis Possum and Sis Dog picked up the kerchief. One little crumb fell out. That kerchief smelled like what it was—empty. Howsoever, truth took over.

"SOMEBODY STOLE OUR CHEESE AND BREAD!" Bruh Bear hollered. Everybody agreed, but what could they do except get madder than a hill of red ants?

Bruh Fox looked down on the ground. "Here some strange-looking tracks," he said, tracing footprints.

"Ain't my tracks," Sis Dog and Sis Possum said, one right behind the other.

"BRUH RABBIT'S TRACKS," Bruh Fox hollered again. "LET'S CATCH HIM AND MAKE HIM PAY!"

"How we gonna catch him?" Sis Possum asked, getting louder. "Bruh Rabbit is as slick as lye soap."

Bruh Fox told them to quiet down. "Bruh Rabbit got good ears," he said. "If we're quiet maybe we can sneak up on him."

Bruh Bear wasn't satisfied with keeping his mouth shut. "Let's sing and hum him out," he said. With that, Bruh Bear fixed his voice and walked toward the thicket, singing. Sis Dog and Sis Possum added their voices. And Bruh Fox laid his mouth open too.

Somebody stole our cheese and bread.
Hmmm, hmmm, hmmm.
He gonna wish he was dead.
I see right there where he dropped a crumb.
Hmmm, hmmm, hmmm.

Bruh Rabbit was just waking up when their voices found his ears. Right away his foot commenced to thumping. He didn't think about the words 'cause the humming tickled his ears so.

See right there where he dropped a crumb.
Hmmm, hmmm, hmmm.
Just about as big as my big thumb.
Somebody stole our cheese and bread.
Hmmm, hmmm, hmmm.

Bruh Rabbit rose up and looked around to see the hummers. That's when Bruh Bear grabbed him 'round the neck. Like I told you: the love of song is what got Bruh Rabbit caught.

"What we gonna do with him?" Sis Dog asked. She hadn't ever heard of anybody catching Bruh Rabbit before.

The more Bruh Bear thought about his hungry stomach, the more ready he was to put a piece of hurtin' on Bruh Rabbit. I'll say this much. Bruh Rabbit had sense enough to keep his mouth shut till he could do some figuring. Well, he couldn't say much no how, the way Bruh Bear had him by the neck.

Bruh Bear led him out of the thicket. Then he plopped Bruh Rabbit on a stump. The four of 'em gathered round.

"What we gonna do with him?" Sis Possum asked.

"Let's drop him in the well!" Bruh Fox said and laughed. "I bet he won't get out of there."

"Oh, thank you, Bruh Fox," Bruh Rabbit spurted out. "I do like cool well water. Y'all gonna drop me in the well?"

"NO!" Bruh Bear hollered.

"How 'bout flinging him in a fire," Sis Possum said, and waited for Bruh Rabbit to jump scared.

Bruh Rabbit turned one eye on Sis Possum and the other eye on Bruh Bear. "Y'all so good to me," he humbled himself. "I been wishing I would get warm at least one time in my life. A good fire would help me out. Y'all gonna fling me in a fire?"

The critters didn't know what to say after that. So Bruh Rabbit decided to help them out as much as he could.

First off, Bruh Rabbit put fear on his face that nobody could wipe off. "Please," he begged. "I know I done y'all wrong. And I know I got to pay for it. But have mercy. Drop me in the well, if you will. Fling me in a fire, if you will. But please, please don't fling me in the briar patch."

Well, the critters commenced to thinking. Bruh Bear and Bruh Fox looked like they wanted to make Bruh Rabbit pay. Sis Possum clapped. Sis Dog just grinned.

Bruh Rabbit put a pitiful catch in his voice and asked, "Y'all gonna fling me in the briar patch?"

"YES!" all of 'em hollered.

Bruh Bear grabbed Bruh Rabbit's legs and Bruh Fox grabbed Bruh Rabbit's ears. They went running to the edge of the briar patch.

Sis Dog and Sis Possum counted the swings: *one, two, three, four.* Bruh Bear and Bruh Fox let go. And Bruh Rabbit went flying through the wind— and landed on his feet.

"Thanky, sirs. Thanky, ma'ams," Bruh Rabbit called out. "This here briar patch is my *home.* Right here, I was bred and *born.*" He settled 'neath a mess of briars.

I ain't seen Bruh Rabbit in a great while. I hear he's still taking whatever comes along and making it his own. He still crazy about good singing too, I reckon.

Oh, I forgot to tell y'all. Bruh Bear, Sis Dog, Bruh Fox, and Sis Possum never did catch Bruh Rabbit any more.

And that's all to it.

This is a story my neighbor Mister Neptune Clark used to tell. We children were not allowed to use the word lie, *but my mother said Mister Nep was the best liar in this whole wide world. Truth for me was that I could picture Bruh Rabbit's briar patch at the edge of the woods with the curled briars waiting to snag whatever passed by.*

Bruh Rabbit talked like everybody in our community. Well, maybe not always, because children had to speak the teacher's language in school. In a sense, we spoke two languages—the teacher's language and the language of Bruh Rabbit.

Bruh Possum & the Snake

We thought trouble was Gramma's most used word. Her warnings to "stay way from trouble, watch out for trouble, take heed, get out from under trouble" and that "trouble can last a long time" were not taken lightly. This story was Gramma's way of teaching us how to get on in the world.

The refrain of her favorite quartet song, sometimes heard at the Great Battle of Songs, was

> *If you don't want,*
> *You don't have to get,*
> *Get in trouble.*
> *You better leave that liar 'lone.*

Bruh Possum was a goodhearted fellow. He always tried to mind his own business. He was a good neighbor, too. If it hadn't been for Bruh Possum, Miss Fox would have lost her youngest, for sure, when he fell in the river. Bruh Possum hung his tail over the bank, and that little fox grabbed hold of it and was saved from drowning.

During the fall, Bruh Possum liked to hang by his tail from the limb of a sweet gum tree. He could sleep hanging upside down all night long. When the frost melted and dried off the grass the next morning, he knew it was time to drop to the ground. Then he headed on down the road to get his breakfast from the persimmon tree. Some of them persimmons were as big as oranges and just as juicy.

One morning, he was on his way to get breakfast. The sun was shining so nice and warm on his body, and he was good and hungry. Pretty soon he saw a great big hole in the middle of the road, just ahead of him. Bruh Possum didn't pay too much mind because he was thinking about his breakfast. He kept on walking, and when he reached the hole he just walked on around it and headed straight down the road again.

All at once Bruh Possum stopped and said to himself, "I didn't even look in that hole in the ground. Wonder if anything was in it—No, I better go on, mind my business and get my breakfast—Wait a minute, I want to know—"

Ole Man Nosy pulled at Bruh Possum's coattail so much so that Bruh Possum made a plan.

"What I'll do is go back, and take a little, bitsy peek. That ain't so nosy." But Ole Man Nosy yanked at his coattail double hard so that when Bruh Possum reached the hole he took a great big look!

There at the bottom of the hole, he saw a big snake with a brick on his back. "Oh, naw!" Bruh Possum whispered as he ducked back. "That's a snake! He ain't nothing but trouble. If he sees me, he'll start snapping and biting and charming me with his beady eyes. And soon I'll be dead." Quiet-like, he inched a few feet back when he heard, "HELP!!"

"Oh, no! He saw me," Bruh Possum cried. "What am I gonna do?"

Well, that old snake begged and begged for Bruh Possum to help him. Bruh Possum was a goodhearted fellow. Trembling, he went back to the hole with his knees knocking together. Then he looked down and asked, "What you want with me?"

The snake's beady eyes never blinked. They just stared up at Bruh Possum while the mouth hissed, "Bruh Pos-s-s-sum, do you s-s-see that brick on my back?"

"Yeah, I see the brick." Bruh Possum panted with fear.

"Take it off for me—will you, please?" he begged.

"Naw! If I take that brick off, you be starting your snapping and biting and charming me with your ugly, beady eyes. And soon I might be dead!"

The snake whispered with a smile, "Maybe not. Maybe not."

Bruh Possum began to wring his hands. "Why didn't I go on 'bout my business when I had the chance?" he said. "Now I don't know what to do! I have to think on it some." He bent his body and thought low. He raised his body and thought high. That's when he spied a dead limb hanging above the hole. In a snap he broke the limb off, stuck it down in the hole, pried that brick off the snake's back, and yonder he ran, *bookety, bookety, bookety, bookety!*

"I got away from him," Bruh Possum squealed. "And he didn't bite me!"

But no sooner had he said that, than he heard, "Help, Bruh Possum, I need you—don't leave me, please—please-s-s-s." The snake was begging pitiful-like from the hole.

"He's calling me again," Bruh Possum moaned. "What am I gonna do now?" He was a goodhearted fellow so he went back and looked in the deep wide hole again. The snake was staring up at him.

"WHY DID YOU CALL ME AGAIN? I TOOK THE BRICK OFF YOUR BACK!" Bruh Possum yelled down.

"I called you 'cause I'm mighty cold down here in this hole," the snake hissed. "Bruh Possum, please take me out of here. Put me on the ditch bank so I feel the nice, warm s-s-sunshine."

Bruh Possum groaned, "You be starting your snapping and biting—I know—"

"Maybe not—maybe not—"

Bruh Possum fretted, "Bruh Snake, you ain't nothing but trouble. I told you and told you 'bout your snapping and biting and charming me."

But he reached down and grabbed the same dead limb. Slowly, he stuck the limb down into the hole and hooked it under the snake's belly. That snake was smiling when Bruh Possum lifted him out. Bruh Possum held that limb as far from himself as he could until he got to the ditch bank. Then, he . . . dropped it! Quick!

And away he ran, *bookety, bookety, bookety, bookety!*

"I got away from him again," Bruh Possum said and laughed. He slowed down to catch his breath. He was so happy. "Now I'll go on and get my breakfast." The sandy road took a turn to the right. The persimmon tree with the juicy, ripe persimmons was 'round the next turn.

Bruh Possum didn't know that snake had been crawling along the ditch bank, right alongside him, until the snake hissed, "Bruh Pos-s-sum, I need you."

Bruh Possum almost jumped out of his shoes. Then he got so mad, he ran over to the ditch bank, shook his finger in the snake's face, and shouted, "I TOOK THE BRICK OFF YOUR BACK! I PUT YOU ON THE DITCH BANK! WHY YOU KEEP CALLIN' ON ME?"

The snake put a sorrowful look on his face. "Bruh Possum, I'm still cold. That's why I called on you. I'm just as cold as I can be. Brrr! Bruh Possum, if you could put . . . me . . . in . . . your . . . pocket . . . I would feel nice and warm for sure. Will you please-s-s-s put me in your pocket?"

Bruh Possum answered, "You got to be crazy."

That snake shivered, but he didn't say another word. Tears dripped from his eyes, and his tongue licked in and out like he was trying to warm his face.

Something in Bruh Possum's chest made him feel sorry for Bruh Snake.

So he grabbed that snake by the tip end of his tail. Ever so gently he rolled the snake to fit into his vest pocket and walked off down the road.

Bruh Possum was satisfied now. The sun was shining full warm on his body. Pretty fall leaves danced about. By 'n' by, he didn't even feel the weight of the snake in his pocket. He thought about those juicy ripe persimmons 'round the next turn in the road.

After a while, Bruh Snake came crawling out of Bruh Possum's pocket. He curled himself 'round to stare in Bruh Possum's face!

"I'm gonna bite you!" he snapped, and hissed.

"You're gonna bite me?" Bruh Possum cried out. "I took the brick off your back. I put you on the ditch bank. I even put you in my pocket so you could get warm! *Now you gonna bite me?*"

The snake spit out, "You knowed I was a s-s-snake when you put me in your pocket!"

And that's why they always say: No matter how good your heart, if you ever spot trouble, don't never trouble trouble if trouble don't trouble you.

And that's all to it.

We jumped every time Gramma made her arm and hand slither out of her apron pocket just like that snake before he pounced into Bruh Possum's face. To me, this story went hand in hand with a verse from my favorite quartet from the Great Battle of Songs:

> *Hypocrite standin' on the corner of the street.*
> *First thing he do is show his feet.*
> *Next thing he do is tell a lie.*
> *Best thing to do is pass him by.*

To Gramma, all snakes were bad. But teachers taught us to recognize a poisonous snake that had a head shaped like three corners. The harmless snake's head was shaped like a circle. I suppose I learned how to spot dishonesty too.

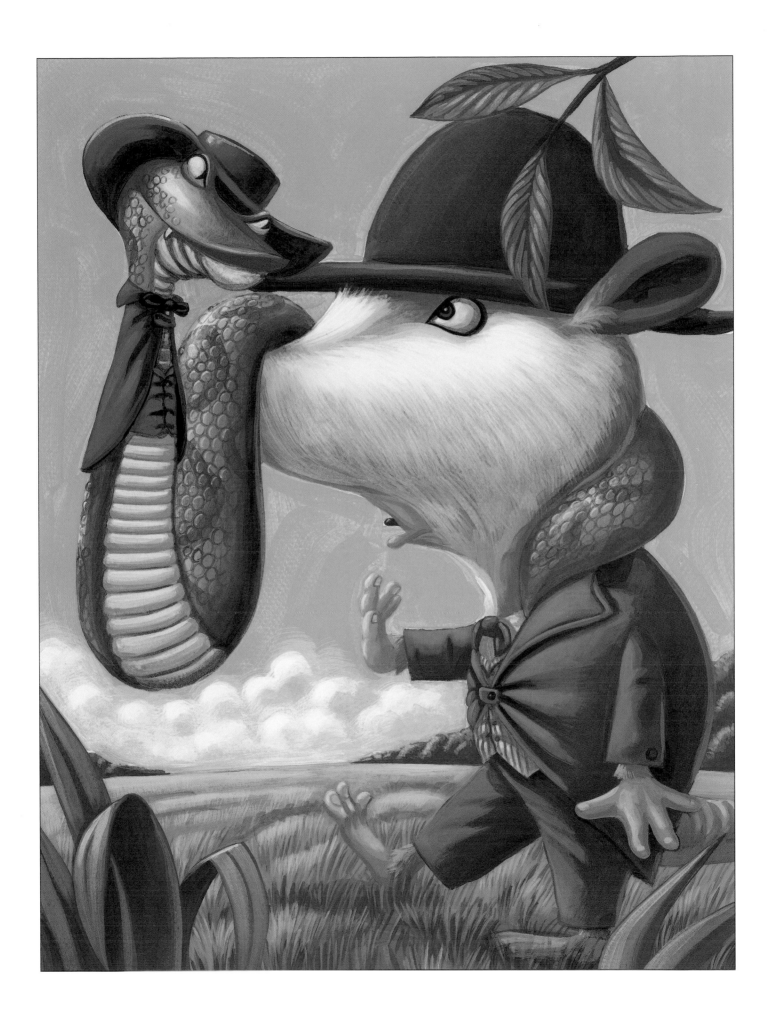

How the Critters Got Groceries

My classmate Derl was in the fifth grade when he told this story to a bunch of us under the shed. We were waiting to see if the rain would slack off enough for us to finish chopping the grass out of a field of cotton on Mister Herbert Whitaker's farm. All of us had heard "How the Critters Got Groceries" before. But Derl kept us in stitches when he acted out the story.

WAY BACK YONDER, FOLKS DIDN'T GO TO STORES TO BUY GROCERIES LIKE they do now. Folks and critters had different ways of getting their food.

Take Bruh Sammy, he was a possum. He got his groceries by taking a crocus sack and a big stick to the swampy pond. Once there, he'd beat the bushes until bullfrogs hopped out. Right quick, Bruh Possum would knock 'em in the head and throw 'em in his sack. His wife and children would be waiting at the house to help him clean the bullfrogs and put salt on their seven days' worth of groceries.

Now, Bruh Cooter, he was a snappin' turtle. Every Saturday morning he'd take his pole and line down to Low River to fish. Oh, he'd catch a whole line of fish. Then, he'd lug 'em home, clean 'em out, and salt 'em down. That's how he put together enough groceries to last him and his family all the week.

Everybody got on fine until Bruh Sammy fell on difficult times. One Saturday, he got about fifteen feet from that pond when a great big bullfrog hopped up on a lily pad and croaked, "HERE HE COME, Y'ALL!"

All them big frogs and all them little frogs jumped in the pond and hid under the water. Bruh Sammy beat at the bushes all 'round the pond. But he could find not one bullfrog. So he took his empty sack on home and told his wife what had happened.

"Well, don't fret 'bout it," she told him. "We got plenty of mush." That's what she fixed to eat all that next week.

Early the next Saturday, Bruh Sammy rushed on down to the pond with his stick and crocus sack. He got within fifteen feet of the pond and tipped the rest of the way so the bullfrogs wouldn't hear him. He got within five feet, still tipping. All at once, a great big bullfrog leaped up on a lily pad and croaked, "HERE HE COME AGAIN, Y'ALL!" Bruh Sammy sprung at the bushes. The frogs hopped in the pond so fast, Bruh Sammy didn't have a chance.

Going back home with no groceries was hard on Bruh Sammy. His wife was sweeping the floor when he told her, "That great big bullfrog jumped up on that lily pad again. I beat the bushes and stirred the water. I couldn't find one bullfrog."

To think of eating mush for seven more days was too much for Bruh Sammy's wife. She didn't mean to harm her husband when she threw the broom. But the broom slammed up against the door facing and bounced right off of Bruh Sammy's forehead.

That thing hurt Bruh Sammy so bad he ran out of the house and headed for the swampy pond again. A knot commenced to growing in the middle of his forehead. Now who was he to meet but Bruh Cooter.

"Hi you be, Bruh Sammy?" Bruh Cooter asked, with his line of fish almost dragging the ground. "You look amighty down in the mouth."

"Look at this knot on my head," Bruh Sammy said. "Wouldn't you be down in the mouth? Lately, every time I go to find my groceries at the pond, a big bullfrog jump up on the lily pad and tell all the frogs, 'HERE HE COME, Y'ALL!' And they all hide from me."

"That be something else," Bruh Cooter said. He kept shifting his eyes 'round, trying to keep from busting out laughing in his friend's face.

Somehow or another, Bruh Cooter collected himself enough to say, "Bruh Sammy, let me think here for a minute. Maybe I can help you."

"What can *you* do?" Bruh Sammy asked.

Bruh Cooter looked Bruh Sammy dead in the eye and pointed to the pond. "Go down to the pond. When you get there, fall flat out dead."

"What you mean telling me to do such a thing?" Bruh Sammy asked.

"I don't mean for you to *die,*" Bruh Cooter said. "I'm saying *pretend* you dead. You a *possum,* ain't you? And don't you move till I get there and say so."

"When you gonna say so?" Bruh Sammy was really worried now.

Bruh Cooter did his best to ease Bruh Sammy's nerves. "Soon as I carry my groceries home to my wife and children, I'll be there. Remember, don't you move." With that, Bruh Cooter cut across the field to his house.

Sure enough, Bruh Sammy went trudging on back to the pond. When that great bullfrog jumped up on the lily pad, Bruh Sammy didn't care. He fell flat out dead on the ground. And he didn't move.

After a while, his back commenced to itching. Bruh Sammy wanted to scratch so bad, but he didn't move. The hot sun dried out his skin and made his belly feel ticklish. He wanted to, at least, smile. But he didn't move. Then, Lawd have mercy, a little ant crawled right across the tip end of Bruh Sammy's nose. Oh, he wanted to twitch, but he didn't move.

By that time, Bruh Cooter was standing over him, crying, "Oh, look at what done happened to my poor friend!"

That same big bullfrog who had been warning all the frogs leaped up on the lily pad and yelled, "WHAT'S THE MATTER WITH HIM?"

"He died." Bruh Cooter wept. "He starved to death."

"WELL, I CAN'T SAY WE SORRY," the frog said. "HE'S BEEN MESSING WITH US A LONG TIME."

"I know," Bruh Cooter moaned. "But now I have to bury—bury him deep. I ain't got nothing to bury him with."

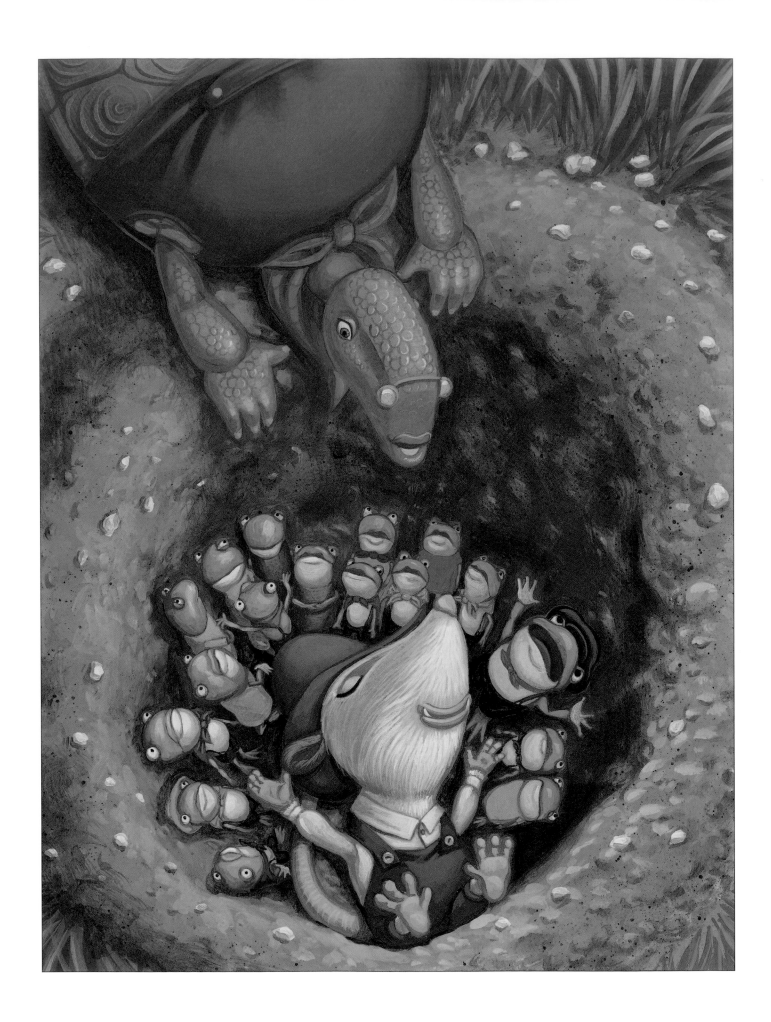

"WE HELP YOU BURY HIM," the frog said in his big loud voice. He called all the little frogs, middle-sized, and big frogs out of the pond and bushes. They made a ring 'round Bruh Sammy and commenced to digging with their feet. Dirt flew everywhere.

After the frogs had sunk Bruh Sammy about three feet into the ground, they rested awhile. Bruh Cooter leaned over the hole. That big bullfrog looked up at Bruh Cooter and asked, "IS IT DEEP ENOUGH?" The little frogs croaked, "IS IT DEEP ENOUGH?"

"Can y'all hop out?" Bruh Cooter asked.

The great big bullfrog checked to see how deep the hole was and said, "YEAH, WE CAN HOP OUT." And the little frogs croaked, "YEAH, WE CAN HOP OUT."

"Well, it ain't deep enough," Bruh Cooter called down.

Them bullfrogs went back to digging and digging. Dirt piled up 'round the hole. It seemed like that hole was about six feet deep when that great big bullfrog stopped to look up and ask Bruh Cooter, "IS IT DEEP ENOUGH? IS IT DEEP ENOUGH?"

"Can y'all hop out?" Bruh Cooter asked, peeping down into the deep wide hole.

That great big bullfrog cut his eyes 'round. "NO, WE CAN'T HOP OUT."

Bruh Cooter hollered down, "WAKE UP, BRUH SAMMY! YOUR GROCERIES IS LAYING ALL 'ROUND YOU!"

Ain't no telling how Bruh Sammy got his groceries after that.

And that's all to it.

My grandmother described Bruh Sammy's victory in this story as "Catch what catch can."

Bruh Rabbit's Mystery Bag

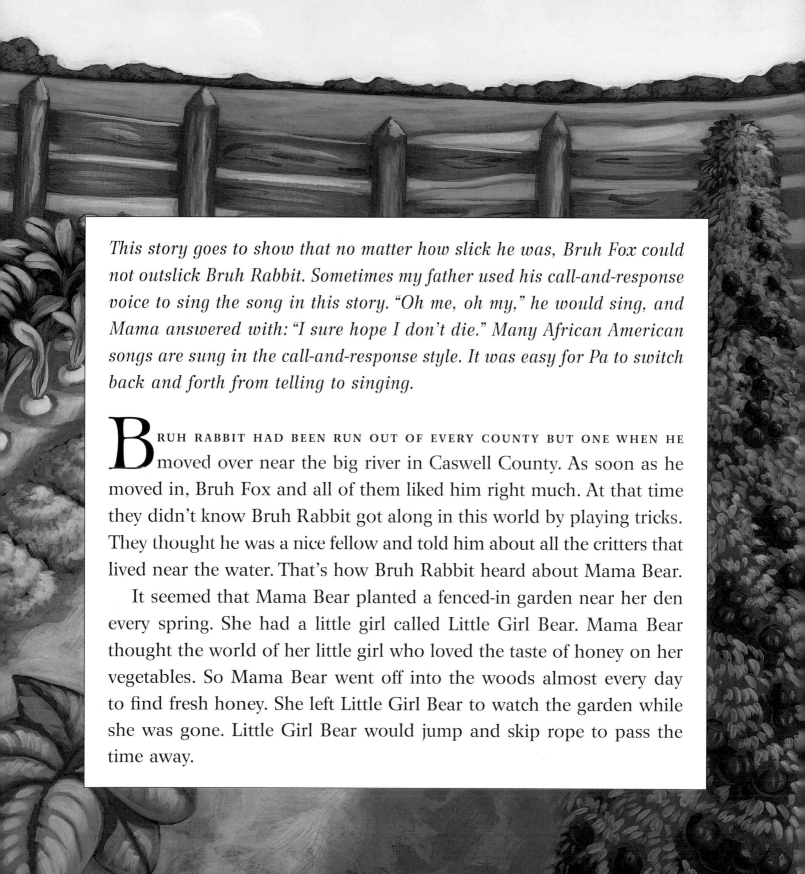

This story goes to show that no matter how slick he was, Bruh Fox could not outslick Bruh Rabbit. Sometimes my father used his call-and-response voice to sing the song in this story. "Oh me, oh my," he would sing, and Mama answered with: "I sure hope I don't die." Many African American songs are sung in the call-and-response style. It was easy for Pa to switch back and forth from telling to singing.

Bruh Rabbit had been run out of every county but one when he moved over near the big river in Caswell County. As soon as he moved in, Bruh Fox and all of them liked him right much. At that time they didn't know Bruh Rabbit got along in this world by playing tricks. They thought he was a nice fellow and told him about all the critters that lived near the water. That's how Bruh Rabbit heard about Mama Bear.

It seemed that Mama Bear planted a fenced-in garden near her den every spring. She had a little girl called Little Girl Bear. Mama Bear thought the world of her little girl who loved the taste of honey on her vegetables. So Mama Bear went off into the woods almost every day to find fresh honey. She left Little Girl Bear to watch the garden while she was gone. Little Girl Bear would jump and skip rope to pass the time away.

One nice warm day when everything in the garden was just about ripe, Bruh Rabbit hopped up, twirling his whiskers. "Little Girl, your mama said let me in the garden," he told her.

Little Girl Bear stopped jumping rope and went straight to the garden gate. Once there, she lifted the latch and opened the gate. Bruh Rabbit hopped on in. She closed the gate, pulled down the latch, and went back to jumping and skipping.

By the time Bruh Rabbit got through eating, his belly was full of a whole head of cabbage and three red-ripe tomatoes. It was about time for him to get out of there. "LITTLE GIRL, YOUR MAMA SAID TO LET ME OUT OF THE GARDEN," he hollered.

Little Girl Bear stopped skipping rope and went to the gate to let Bruh Rabbit out. He hopped back into the woods, whistling.

Bruh Rabbit went back to that garden so many more times, the critters noticed that he was putting on weight. That was about all they noticed because springtime was such a busy time of year. New young ones had to get born, and new mouths had to be fed. Bruh Cooter fussed at his little snapping turtles day and night trying to keep them from swimming off in high water. One of Sis Possum's young ones fell on his head at least once a day, trying to learn how to hang upside down by his tail like all good possums. So nobody noticed Bruh Rabbit eating out of Mama Bear's garden.

Not caring how much his stomach stuck out, Bruh Rabbit just couldn't get enough of the taste of those delicious vegetables. So he kept telling Little Girl Bear to let him in the garden.

At last, one day, Mama Bear missed so many turnips, tomatoes, and cabbages, she called Little Girl Bear to the gate. "Did you eat out of the garden while I was looking for honey?"

"No, Mama," the little bear answered.

"You been watching the garden like I told you?"

"Yes, Mama."

"Then why so many cabbages be missing? Look like somebody been here."

"When you go to get honey," Little Girl Bear told her mama, "Bruh Rabbit

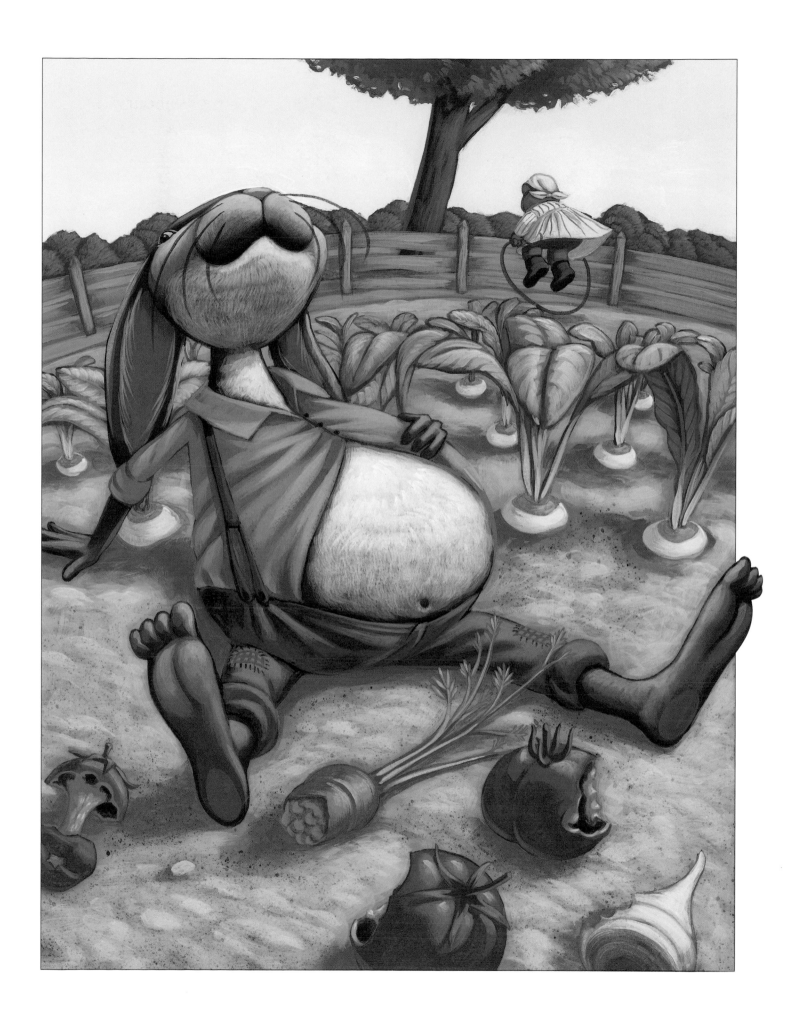

comes out of the woods and tells me, 'Little Girl, your mama said to let me in the garden.' I let him in, and he eats and eats. Then he hollers, 'LITTLE GIRL, YOUR MAMA SAID TO LET ME OUT OF THE GARDEN,' and I let him out."

Mama Bear thought long and hard before she said, "Next time Bruh Rabbit wants to eat from the garden I want you to let him in, but don't let him out. Keep him here till I get back."

As sure as sunrise, Bruh Rabbit came hippety-hopping out of the woods the very next day. He was as hungry as he was in a hurry. "Little Girl, stop that jumping rope. Your mama said to let me in the garden."

Little Girl Bear let her rope fall on the ground. She ran to the garden gate and lifted up the latch. Bruh Rabbit hopped in like before, but this time he looked over his shoulder at Little Girl Bear like he was the boss of the whole world and reminded her, "Pull the latch down." So she did.

Instead of eating one head of cabbage, Bruh Rabbit ate two. He mowed down a row of lettuce with his teeth. He ate four tomatoes and a whole lot of bunch beans. His belly was dragging on the ground. He was just able to yell out, "LITTLE GIRL, YOUR MAMA SAID TO LET ME OUT OF THE GARDEN."

Little Girl Bear kept skipping rope like she hadn't ever heard tell of Bruh Rabbit. That's when Bruh Rabbit got a feeling that something was about to happen. Just then, Mama Bear ran to the gate and looked a straight eye at Bruh Rabbit.

"How you be doing, Miss Bear?" Bruh Rabbit grinned at her while he scrunched down to dig himself a hole. He was too late. His heart almost fluttered out of his mouth when Mama Bear reached over the gate, grabbed him by his ears, and dropped him in a sack. Bruh Rabbit couldn't see nothing, but he sure could hear Mama Bear hollering, "BRUH RABBIT, I'M HANGING THIS SACK UP A TREE. THEN I'M GONNA BREAK ME SOME LONG, LIMBER SWITCHES AND BRING THEM BACK HERE." Then he heard Mama Bear stomp away.

Bruh Rabbit could feel himself swinging between earth and sky. His nerves

just 'bout gave out on him. "Oh me, oh my, here I hang b'twix earth and sky."
He tried to sing up some courage. "Oh me, oh my, I sure hope I don't die."

"WHO THAT UP THERE?" somebody on the ground hollered.

"Who that down there?" Bruh Rabbit asked, twitching around in the sack.

"Who that up there saying 'WHO THAT?' when I say 'WHO THAT?'"
the same voice came back to Bruh Rabbit.

"Bruh Fox, is that you?" Bruh Rabbit asked, feeling glad-happy.

"It's me all right." Bruh Fox snickered. "What you doing up a tree, swinging and singing a sad song?" He had a feeling Bruh Rabbit was in a heap
of trouble.

"Well, I tell you, Bruh Fox, I found this mystery bag," Bruh Rabbit said.
"I just figured out what'll make it work. All sorts of good-tasting vittles up in
here. Some of the best-roasted chicken legs you ever tasted." With that, Bruh
Rabbit commenced to chewing and smacking his lips.

"Yeah, how big?" Bruh Fox asked, not quite believing Bruh Rabbit.

"This big," Bruh Rabbit said and poked his elbow in the corner of the bag.
Bruh Fox leaped up and felt the elbow, thinking it was a chicken leg. His
watering mouth made him beg, "Bruh Rabbit, you know me 'n' you and me
be good friends. Throw me down just one chicken leg."

"That ain't the way this mystery bag works," Bruh Rabbit said, still chewing
and smacking. "You got to loosen the bag and when I hop out, you hop in."

Bruh Fox was so greedy, he jumped on the limb and loosened the rope
and the top of the sack. Then he and Bruh Rabbit passed each other—one
coming out and the other going in. By the time Bruh Fox hit the bottom of
that bag, he knew he'd been tricked. When he hollered out to Bruh Rabbit a
few times, he didn't get no answer. You see, Mama Bear was rounding the tree
with her long, limber switches. Bruh Rabbit was running away when Mama
Bear commenced to beating that sack. KAPOW! KAPOW! KAPOW!

Then Mama Bear stopped beating and let the bag fall to the ground so
the one she thought was Bruh Rabbit could find his way out.

Bruh Fox never did say a word to nobody 'bout the mystery sack, less they
thought him the fool. But he'd break out in the shamefaced grins whenever

he was in the company of Bruh Rabbit. I reckon Bruh Rabbit stayed away from Mama Bear's garden after that. Or did he? Anyhow, Bruh Fox still can't stand Bruh Rabbit.

And that's all to it.

When I was a child Bruh Rabbit made me think a good trick was the same as a good laugh. So one day I unscrewed the hinges off of my grandmother's trunk top. When she opened the trunk, the top fell on the floor with a loud bang. I had a good laugh—for a little while. Then, I didn't know what made me do such a thing because I got punished for sure. I have not misused a screwdriver since then—over fifty years ago.

Looking to Get Married

When I was growing up, the king in this story reminded me of a heavyset storekeeper named Mister Harvey Hardtime. He was true to his name by giving me a hard time one day when I entered his store to buy a pencil and notebook paper. "Somebody like you don't need pencils and paper," he said in his meanest voice. "Buy yourself a bar of candy." Afraid, I accepted the candy bar but my mother escorted me back to the store. She had fire in her eyes. Mister Harvey's face turned red when my mother demanded that he take back the candy bar. He returned the ten cents but refused to sell her the pencil and paper. He thought I should learn to work in the field, not learn to read and write. We never went to that store again. I thought my mother was the bravest woman I had ever seen.

BRUH RABBIT WAS A BAD MAMMAJAMMA. THAT MEANT HE HAD PLUCK. HE wasn't a bit more scared of the king than he was of a little biddy flea. But all the other critters trembled every time they took a look up the hill where the king lived in a big brick house.

Any time of day, the king looked down below and saw all the scared critters working his fields and woods. They worked for him and they didn't get paid. Bruh Possum and his family worked for free. Bruh Bully

Frog and his wife did the same. Sis Bear had two little ones working alongside her. Bruh Cooter had a mighty big family that worked and never got a cent. That king had so many critters working for free, he couldn't even count all of them.

Bruh Rabbit wouldn't think of working for free, not even for the king. But no matter how many times he tried to encourage the critters to stand strong, they couldn't listen.

One sunny morning, Bruh Rabbit was sitting beside the road among tall broom straw when the critters straggled by on their way to another field. They looked so pitiful.

"DON'T WORK FOR THE KING IF HE AIN'T PLANNING ON PAYING YOU," Bruh Rabbit hollered out. "BE LIKE ME. I DON'T WORK FOR FREE."

"We can't be like you, Bruh Rabbit." Sis Possum was the only one who wasn't too scared to answer back. "Our young ones need looking after. Leastways, we got somewhere to stay and something to eat every once in a while." She cut her eyes up at the king's house. Good thing he wasn't in the yard. She tottered on as fast as she could.

Bruh Rabbit nuzzled down in a wide clump of broom straw and chewed on a stalk of grass. Seem like the critters just wouldn't listen to him. Pretty soon he dozed off.

Before long, a *clippety-cloppety* noise roused Bruh Rabbit. He sat up and peered down the road at four big white prancing horses pulling a gray carriage with silver trimmings. Soon Bruh Rabbit could see inside. There sat the king with a crown on his big round head. Sitting beside the king, with a little crown on her head, was the prettiest girl-critter in the world. Bruh Rabbit was sure of that because the sight of her made wedding tunes chime through his mind. "I wanta marry her," he said out loud after the prancing horses pulled the carriage around the bend in the road. "That's what I'm gonna do, too. And right after the wedding, I can help all the critters get free or get paid."

Bruh Rabbit was getting ahead of himself right then. How was he going to ask for the pretty girl-critter's hand in marriage? Oh, he tramped and twisted 'round in that broom straw till quit-work time at the end of the day. Nothing but the wedding tune had come to his mind. "I'll go tell Bruh Fox and Bruh Bully Frog 'bout my plan. They might think of something if I ask all the critters to my wedding to-do."

The critters were hanging around their little huts when Bruh Rabbit strolled up. "Brothers, brothers," he called the menfolk critters to gather 'round him. "I'm looking to get married."

"Oh, Lawd," Bruh Bully Frog croaked.

"Hope he don't wanna marry my daughter," Bruh Possum said.

The whispered word was passed around that if anyone allowed Bruh Rabbit to marry his daughter, she was liable to starve to death.

Bruh Rabbit got madder and madder by the second. "I DON'T WANT TO MARRY YOUR DAUGHTERS!" he yelled. "THEY UGLY. I'M GONNA MARRY THE KING'S DAUGHTER!"

Did the critters carry on about how crazy Bruh Rabbit was, thinking he could marry the king's daughter? Yes they did. Bruh Fox even snuck off up the hill to the king's house and knocked on the door.

"WHAT ARE YOU DOING KNOCKING AT MY DOOR?" the king's big, tall voice bellowed out.

"I'm here to warn you, Mister King." Bruh Fox panted. "Bruh Rabbit is looking to marry your daughter." Bruh Fox stepped back, right pleased with himself. He never could stand Bruh Rabbit's tricky ways.

"YOU GO BACK DOWN THAT HILL AND GET YOURSELF READY FOR WORK TOMORROW!" The king's shout sent Bruh Fox tumbling off the porch.

By the next morning, Bruh Rabbit had figured out what to do. The wedding tune still danced in his mind. He dressed in his polished lace-up shoes and his yellow waistcoat with the watch chain dangling down. Then he laid his ears back and went high-stepping to the king's house. The king heard Bruh Rabbit's *tap-tap-tap-tap-tap-tap* at his door.

"What you want?" the king asked as the door swung open.

"Good morning, Bruh King," Bruh Rabbit spoke kindly, thinking he could soften up the king by calling him Bruh.

"Good morning to you, Bruh Rabbit," the king said.

"I come up to ask you something."

"What is it?"

"I'm asking for your daughter's hand in marriage."

"Fine."

Bruh Rabbit got speechless with happiness. "I sure didn't know 'twas this easy," he said under his breath.

Then the king held up his hand, and added, "Before you marry my daughter,

you must do as I ask." With that, the king handed a big burlap bag to Bruh Rabbit. "Take this bag wherever you want to, but bring it back to me filled up with blackbirds."

Bruh Rabbit worried over trying to catch blackbirds, but he was smiling as he turned away, saying, "I can do that 'fore sundown."

"Wait!" the king said, pulling a little drawstring bag from his pocket. He handed this little bag to Bruh Rabbit. "I want you to bring this bag back with two rattlesnake's teeth in it."

Bruh Rabbit was scared to death of snakes, especially rattlesnakes. But, again, he smiled, and said, "I can do that 'fore sundown. When can I plan on getting married?"

"After that," the king said, watching Bruh Rabbit fold the bags. "You will have to do one more thing. Then you can marry my daughter."

Bruh Rabbit had made his way to the bottom of the hill before a trick came to his mind. He rushed into the woods and sat down under a big oak tree where all the blackbirds hung out. He commenced to sing.

> *Blackbirds so skinny,*
> *Quail birds so fat,*
> *Blackbirds so skinny,*
> *Quail birds so fat.*

Blackbirds swooped out of the branches and pecked at Bruh Rabbit's ears, complaining, "We just as fat as quail birds. Look here," they bragged, and fluffed up their feathers.

"I don't believe you," Bruh said, spreading his bag open. "Fly in this bag, and I'll weigh you. Then I'll weigh some quail birds. That'll tell me who's fatter."

The birds flew right in, and Bruh Rabbit tied a string around the bag and pulled it alongside him deeper into the woods.

After a while, he spotted one of the biggest, coiled-up rattlesnakes he had ever seen in his natural-born days. That snake appeared to be sleeping. Bruh

Rabbit whispered, ready to jump and run. "Bruh Snake, I come to bring you some bad news."

The snake cracked open one eye, and hissed, "S-s-swhat bad news-s-s-s?"

Bruh Rabbit whispered back, "Well, the word is out that you got a crooked back. I'm here to see if that's so. If it ain't, I'll go back and set critters straight."

Without a word, that snake commenced to uncoil itself. "S-s-see," the snake hissed. "My back is-s s-not crooked."

"You right. Your back ain't crooked," Bruh Rabbit said, standing in front of the snake's head. "But I think your teeth look crooked. Open your mouth."

As soon as the snake opened his mouth, Bruh Rabbit took the heel of his hand and bopped out two teeth. As quick as lightning, he dropped them into the little drawstring bag, grabbed the burlap bag of birds, and scrambled back to the king's house. He laid the bags at the king's feet.

"He's good," the king said to himself, letting the birds go and stuffing the teeth into his pocket.

"What's next?" Bruh Rabbit asked with the wedding tune in his mind.

The king reached 'round the door and struggled to pull the last bag to the door. After some time, he loaded it on Bruh Rabbit's back, and said, "Take this bag of money and bury it. When you come back, tell me where you buried it. Then you can marry my daughter."

"I can do that 'fore sundown," Bruh Rabbit said. He heaved the load off the porch, bent double. By the time Bruh Rabbit reached the bottom of the hill, he had to ease that bag off his back to catch his breath. All at once, the thought hit him. "I ain't got no wedding suit!" he said, straightening his body. "Oh," he said to himself, laughing. "I know what to do. I'll just take enough money out'n this bag to buy me a nice suit. After I marry the king's daughter, I can pay him back."

He untied the string and poked his hand in to grab a fist full of money. That's when three great big hound dogs jumped out! Those dogs chased Bruh Rabbit out of the county. He never did marry the king's daughter.

He kept sneaking back to help the critters get free of the king, though. Up until this day, Bruh Rabbit is still not married. If you are a pretty girl and if

you hear a knock on your door like this—*tap-tap-tap-tap-tap-tap*—peep out the window before you open the door. It could be Bruh Rabbit. He's still looking for a wife.

And that's all to it.

As a child, I wanted Bruh Rabbit to marry the king's daughter. Then he would have been happy, ever after, as in fairy tales. That Bruh Rabbit never gave up echoed my mother's encouraging words, "If you keep on keeping on, you will get there." Bookety, bookety, bookety!